HAPPY
Birthday
imagination

Happy birthday, Puffin!

D ! you know that in 1940 the very first Puffin story
b k (about a man with broomstick arms called Worzel
G nmidge) was published? That's 70 years ago! Since then
tl little Puffin logo has become one of the most recognized
b k brands in the world and Puffin has established its
p ce in the hearts of millions.

A 1 in 2010 we are celebrating 70 spectacular years of
1 'fin and its books! Pocket Money Puffins is a brand-new
lection from your favourite authors at a pocket-money
ce – in a perfect pocket size. We hope you enjoy these
citing stories and we hope you'll join us in celebrating
e very best books for children. We may be 70 years old
ounds ancient, doesn't it?) but Puffin has never been so
ely and fun.

There really IS a Puffin book for everyone
– discover yours today.

Jeremy Strong once worked in a bakery, putting the jam into three thousand doughnuts every night. Now he puts the jam in stories instead, which he finds much more exciting. At the age of three, he fell out of a first-floor bedroom window and landed on his head. His mother says that this damaged him for the rest of his life and refuses to take any responsibility. He loves writing stories because he says it is 'the only time you alone have complete control and can make anything happen'. His ambition is to make you laugh (or at least snuffle). Jeremy Strong lives near Bath with his wife, Gillie, four cats and a flying cow.

Are you feeling silly enough to read more?

LAUGH YOUR Socks off with

Jeremy STRONG

We Want to be on the Telly!

Illustrated by
Rowan Clifford

PUFFIN

PUFFIN BOOKS

Published by the Penguin Group
Penguin Books Ltd, 80 Strand, London WC2R ORL, England
Penguin Group (USA) Inc., 375 Hudson Street, New York, New York 10014, USA
Penguin Group (Canada), 90 Eglinton Avenue East, Suite 700, Toronto, Ontario, Canada M4P 2Y3
(a division of Pearson Penguin Canada Inc.)
Penguin Ireland, 25 St Stephen's Green, Dublin 2, Ireland (a division of Penguin Books Ltd)
Penguin Group (Australia), 250 Camberwell Road, Camberwell, Victoria 3124, Australia
(a division of Pearson Australia Group Pty Ltd)
Penguin Books India Pvt Ltd, 11 Community Centre, Panchsheel Park, New Delhi – 110 017, India
Penguin Group (NZ), 67 Apollo Drive, Rosedale, North Shore 0632, New Zealand
(a division of Pearson New Zealand Ltd)
Penguin Books (South Africa) (Pty) Ltd, 24 Sturdee Avenue, Rosebank,
Johannesburg 2196, South Africa

Penguin Books Ltd, Registered Offices: 80 Strand, London WC2R ORL, England

puffinbooks.com

First published 2010
1

Text copyright © Jeremy Strong, 2010
Illustration copyright © Rowan Clifford, 2010
Colour Puffin artwork on cover copyright © Jill McDonald, 1974
All rights reserved

The moral right of the author and illustrator has been asserted

Set in Adobe Caslon 14.25/28 pt
Typset by Ellipsis Book Production Limited, Glasgow
Made and printed in England by Clays Ltd, St Ives plc

British Library Cataloguing in Publication Data
A CIP catalogue record for this book is available from the British Library

ISBN: 978-0-141-32818-8

www.greenpenguin.co.uk

Penguin Books is committed to a sustainable future
for our business, our readers and our planet.
The book in your hands is made from paper
certified by the Forest Stewardship Council.

This little story is dedicated to Puffin Books.
Thank you for all the wonderful tales and
amazing picture books you have given to us all
over many years. You have been an inspiration for
our dreams as children and our lives as adults,
broadening our awareness and being a happy
part of what many of us have become.

J. S.

Contents

The Baby Now Arriving at London Airport

It started at breakfast.

'We're going to be on the telly,' said Mum. Dad stood behind her, grinning as if he'd just won a million pounds AND free chocolate for the rest of his life.

'Really?' I said. 'On TV? What for?'

'Don't know,' said Mum. 'We haven't

decided yet. The thing is, your pa and I have always wanted to be on the telly and now we're going to do it.' (Mum always calls my dad 'Pa' and Dad always calls my mum 'Ma'. Don't ask me why. I haven't a clue.)

'We'll be famous,' said Dad. 'We'll walk down the street and people will look at us and point and say, "Look! It's Pa and Ma off the telly!" We'll be famous,' he repeated.

'But people look at you anyway,' I pointed out.

It's true. People always stare at my

parents because, to be honest, they are

VERY STRANGE. They like to sport

giant sunglasses and put on silly hats. Dad

wears trousers that are too short and socks that don't match. Mum's got one of those trick arrows that looks as if it's gone right through her head.

People stop them in the street and say: 'Why are you dressed like that?' And do you know what my parents say?

'It's fun!'

NO, IT ISN'T! STOP DOING IT!
YOU JUST LOOK STUPID!
AND YOU MAKE *ME*
FEEL STUPID TOO!

Why can't my mum and dad just be ORDINARY? You can imagine what it's like when I go to school. The other children are always pestering me.

'Heathrow, your parents are total bonker-plonkers.' That's the sort of thing they say. It's not nice, is it?

And imagine what it's like when Mum and Dad come to school for parent-teacher interviews! Dad sits there with a pretend axe stuck in his head while Mum wears plastic Dracula fangs and has fake blood dribbling from the corners of her mouth.

Even my teacher, Mr Jollop, asks questions, and he reckons he's seen everything. (We know this because he's always shaking his head at our schoolwork and saying: 'Now I've seen everything.') Anyhow, even Mr Jollop has started asking questions.

'Heathrow, your parents . . . um . . .?' His voice trailed away, his eyebrows knitted themselves into half a sock, and he looked confused.

'Yes?' I said helpfully.

'Your parents, are they . . . um . . .?'

'Mad?' I suggested.

'Oh, oh, not exactly, no, not mad, just a bit . . . um . . .?'

'Off this planet and possibly somewhere in an entirely different universe altogether?' I offered.

'Oh, oh, no, no, I wouldn't go that far. It's . . . it's . . . it's just they're a bit . . . um?'

'Weird?' I prompted.

'Oh, oh,' Mr Jollop began, his eyes as round as his oh-oh-oh-ing mouth.

'Weird? Hmmmm. Well, yes, in a way, weird might be the um . . . the word. Yes, in a word, weird IS the word. Hmm.' And his eyebrows knitted the rest of the sock.

So as you can see most people think my parents are strange.

By the way, in case you're wondering why I'm called Heathrow, you can blame my parents again. When they got married, they used to spend every Sunday having afternoon tea at the café in the Arrivals area at London Heathrow Airport. They used to try to spot famous people arriving.

My mum was getting fatter and fatter. She thought it was all the cakes she was eating at the café. Then one Sunday she came over all faint and before they knew it she was giving birth – to me! I was born in the Arrivals area of a major London airport. That's why they called me Heathrow. My life has been going downhill ever since.

Now they want to be on the telly. That means that soon the WHOLE WORLD will know how strange my parents are. I sat there at breakfast and my heart turned into one of those small, cold, unidentifiable splobs you

find lurking at the back of a fridge.
It's been there for three years, going
mouldy, and nobody can remember
what it was.

Mum and Dad stood beside the
breakfast table, smiling and grinning
with excitement. 'On the telly!' Dad cried.
'Isn't that wonderful!'

And my heart cried out inside me:
'No, Dad. It's not wonderful. I don't
want everyone to know how daft you can
be. I just want you to be normal and
ordinary. I'd like to be able to look at you

without wanting to curl up and get back into the fridge.'

But it's not going to happen, is it?

2

Anyone for a Bath?

My parents' first idea was that they would spend the rest of their lives living in the bath. Now then, we have quite a large bathroom and quite a big bath, but even so it's not the sort of thing you might choose to spend the rest of your life in.

Personally speaking, I like baths. I prefer a bath to a shower. When you have a bath, you can play submarines. You can curl your fingers into a fist and turn your hand into a water pistol and squirt people. You can slide down beneath the surface of the water and see how long you can hold your breath.

And, best of all, if by any chance you happen to – excuse my language – let one off, and I'm sure you know what I mean, it makes the most amazing underwater explosion of bubbles. Which then burst

on the surface and poison you with

horrible gas.

You can't do any of those things when

you have a shower. Baths are definitely

better. But would you want to live in a bath tub? I don't think so.

'Will there be water in the bath?' I asked.

'Of course!' Dad grinned.

'Will you both be in the bath at the same time?' I enquired.

'Yes!' Mum beamed.

'And you are going to eat and sleep and work in the bath?'

'Exactly!' said Dad. 'And you are going to bring us breakfast and lunch and supper.'

'I see. But if you're in the bath, won't you be – you know? Or will you make sure it's a bubble bath – with an awful lot of bubbles?' I added hastily, turning as red as a tomato with no knickers.

'Silly boy,' laughed Mum. 'We'll be keeping our clothes on, of course.'

'Of course,' I echoed. 'You'll be keeping your clothes on. In the bath. How stupid of me to imagine you might have taken them off.'

Dad burst into hysterical giggles. 'Not on telly, Heathrow. Don't be daft!' And there you have it. My dad was going to live in a bath full of water, with all his clothes on, and with Mum there too, and he was telling ME not to be daft. I was still shaking my head at this when Mum said they were going to run the bath straight away.

'So you must ring up the telly people and tell them what we're doing,' she added.

'Must I?'

'Yes.'

Mum and Dad disappeared upstairs.

A few moments later I heard water running. I gave a big sigh and went to the telephone.

The telly people were not very helpful. They wanted to know how long my parents had been living in the bath. I looked at the clock.

'About five minutes,' I answered.

'Tell them to get back to us in a year,' said the woman from the telly, and she put the phone down. When I told Mum and Dad what had happened, they weren't the least bit put out.

'We can easily manage a year, can't we, Ma?' said Dad, resting his feet (with socks and shoes) on Mum's shoulders. 'Ring the newspaper people instead and tell them what we're doing. They're

bound to send a photographer and when the telly people see the photo they'll come and film us. In the meantime, could you bring me today's paper and a cup of coffee?'

'And I'll have a cup of tea and a biscuit,' added Mum, giving a little wriggle. 'I've been sitting on the soap,' she chuckled. 'I thought it felt a bit uncomfortable.'

I heaved another sigh and went down to the kitchen. While the kettle boiled, I rang the local newspaper. They were not very helpful either. In fact they just laughed and asked me if my surname was Fish. Or maybe Trout? Or Haddock? Mr and Mrs Sardine? The Kipper family, perhaps? Jack Sprat? Squid?

'The squid isn't a fish,' I pointed out coldly, and put the phone down. I finished making the drinks and went up to the bathroom with the bad news.

'Never mind,' said Dad, 'I have another idea. You get a bed sheet, Heathrow, and a black felt-tip pen. Write on it with extra-big letters:

COME AND SEE US LIVING
IN OUR BATH!

Hang it from the front bedroom
window and soon people will be queuing
up to watch. The telly people are certain
to come and see what all the fuss is
about.'

My jaw just about fell off. In fact
I'm pretty sure it bounced on the floor a
couple of times before going back into
place. Did my parents really want the
whole street queuing up outside to see

them being prize nincompoops? I didn't

bother to ask them because I knew the

answer was 'YES!'

I went trudging off to the linen

cupboard and pulled out a big white

sheet. I took it downstairs and spread

it across the floor in the front room.

I stomped up to my bedroom and found

a big fat felt-tip pen. I trudged back

downstairs, slumped down in front of the

sheet and took the top off the pen.

I was about to start writing when

there was a double scream from upstairs.

'AAAAARGH!'

'EEUUURRGH!'

I rushed back up. Dad was writhing
about, clutching his left thigh.

'I've got cramp from being in the
same position for too long. It's agony!'
he cried.

'And Pa's jerking about made me stick
my big toe up the cold tap and now it's
stuck!' added Mum.

'Help us!' they chorused.

I looked at them struggling. I folded

my arms. 'I'll help you on one condition,' I said.

'Anything, we'll do anything!' they pleaded.

'You've got to give up this idea of living in the bath.'

'Yes! Yes!' Dad agreed at once. 'Just get me out so I can walk around and ease this awful cramp.'

I helped Dad climb from the tub and he squelched off, up and down the hall, shaking his left leg and leaving puddles everywhere. I managed to push some soap up the sides of Mum's big toe until she could slip it from the tap. Then she got out and made big squelchy puddles everywhere too.

I didn't care. My parents had given up on their crazy idea. Hooray. Maybe things would go back to normal now.

Fat chance.

3

Anyone for Rice Pudding?

'The trouble with the bath was that it wasn't big enough, Heathrow,' Dad explained the next day.

'Yes,' agreed Mum, nodding. 'And it wasn't interesting enough for the telly people either. So your pa has come up with the most marvellous plan. We're going to live in the garden pond instead.'

I wanted to close my ears. I wanted to close my eyes. I wanted to find myself a million miles away. But of course I didn't.

'And that's not all,' Dad added.

'It isn't?' I asked, my voice weak, dreading what he might say next.

'No,' said Dad. 'The pond won't have any water in it.'

That didn't sound too bad. I perked up a bit. 'No water? At least you'll stay dry, then.'

'Not exactly,' Mum smiled. 'We're going to fill it with rice pudding.'

GULP!

'Rice pudding?' I squeaked.

'It will be the biggest rice pudding in the world,' said Dad.

'And we'll be sitting right in the middle of it,' added Mum.

'With your clothes on, I suppose?' I asked.

Dad shook his head. 'Ma's going to

wear her bikini and I shall be in my swimming trunks.'

'And a snorkel. Don't forget your snorkel and face mask. I thought that was a really good idea. Nobody will expect to find someone living in a pond full of rice pudding and wearing a snorkel.'

'Exactly,' laughed Dad. 'Your ma's as bright as a button, Heathrow!'

And secretly I was thinking: *No, she isn't! My mum's as daft as – as daft as someone who sits in rice pudding wearing their swimsuit.*

Now, our pond was not a thing of beauty. About the only thing that made it a pond was that it had water in it. There were no fish or frogs. There were no water snails. There were no beautiful water lilies. There wasn't even a shopping trolley. In fact the only thing in the pond, apart from water, was a large, dead gnome.

It was one of those statue things you find in garden centres. It was supposed to be a fountain, with water squishing out of the top of the gnome's hat. However,

Dad's never been much good at that Do-It-Yourself stuff. He had never got the fountain to work and eventually it just fell over, face down in the middle of the pond, and Dad left it there.

By mid-morning my parents had drained the pond of water and pulled the gnome on to the grass.

'I think it needs the Kiss of Life,' joked Dad.

'Time to get the rice pudding,' Mum said. 'Come on, Heathrow. You can help.'

'Oh good,' I said, with no enthusiasm whatsoever.

We went to one of those bulk-buy supermarkets – the sort of place restaurants get their food supplies from. We bought catering-size tins of rice pudding. Do you know how big a catering-size tin of rice pudding is? It's the same size as a large bucket, a bucket full, *full*, of rice pudding. Mum and Dad bought thirty tins. THIRTY! Plus a heavy-duty tin opener.

Back at the house they got to work

and were soon tipping one tin after

another into the pond.

'It looks great,' said Dad.

'Lovely,' said Mum.

'Lumpy,' I muttered as they went

indoors to change. When they came

back out, Mum was wearing a yellow

polka-dot bikini, sunglasses and carrying

a deckchair. Dad had his trunks on,

plus his snorkel and face mask, as

promised. He'd also found an old pair

of rubber flippers.

They waded into the pond.

'Urrgh,' went Mum. 'It's a bit –'

'Lumpy?' I suggested.

'Cold,' she corrected, setting up her

deckchair and plonking her bottom on it.

Dad chose to lie near the edge, idly

kicking his flippered feet and flicking rice
pudding into the air.

'OK, Heathrow,' he said. 'Get on that
phone to the telly people.'

I went indoors with a heavy heart.

It was the same woman I had spoken
to before. 'I told you last time, it has to be
for at least a year. Then we might be
interested.'

I didn't bother to tell my parents.
I knew what they would say so I rang
the newspapers next.

'Are their heads poking out or are

they living beneath the rice pudding?'
asked the man at the other end of the
phone.

'They're not deep-rice-pudding
divers,' I answered crossly. 'Of course their
heads are poking out.'

A disappointed grunt came from the
phone. 'Shame. We had someone in a
giant rice pudding last month. They had
their heads sticking out too. We don't
need another one. Can't you ask your
parents to pop their heads underneath
and stay there?'

'If they did that, they wouldn't be able to breathe,' I snapped. 'And you wouldn't be able to see them either so what would be the point in taking a picture?'

'Good thinking,' answered the man. 'No point at all, so no picture. Goodbye.' The phone went dead. It was just as well, otherwise I might have ended up with two parents AND a gnome, all in need of the Kiss of Life.

I went and told Mum and Dad. Funnily enough they didn't seem all that disappointed.

'What many people don't realize
is that rice pudding makes you itch,'
said Dad.

'Especially when it gets inside your
bikini,' added Mum, scratching herself all
over. 'And it's also rather clammy,' Dad
muttered.

They got to their feet. Mum
folded her deckchair. They held each
other by the hand and slopped up to
the house. Dad threw a sad glance
back at the pond. 'Shame about that,'
he said. 'Never mind. We're bound to

think of something to get us on the
telly.'

'Bound to,' said Mum brightly.
'I can't wait.'

I can, I thought. *I can wait forever.*

4

What's Large, Pink and Flies Backwards?

'I saw a picture once of a house with a shark sticking out of the roof,' said Dad, that same afternoon.

'Did you, Pa?' asked Mum.

'I did. It was in a newspaper. It wasn't the local paper. It was in a NATIONAL paper.' Dad nodded hard to show how impressed he was. 'The shark was poking right out of the roof as if it was leaping into the sky.'

'A house with a shark on the roof,' Mum repeated slowly, chewing the idea as if it was a nice big lump of roast chicken, with gravy. 'Have we got a shark, Pa?' she asked.

I wanted to stick my fingers in my ears. What kind of person asks a question like that? What did Mum think Dad would say? *Yes, dear, there's a fully grown shark in the fridge. I'm surprised you didn't notice. I'll just get it out and pop it on the roof.*

Dad shook his head. 'No, we haven't, Ma. But maybe we can get one. I'll take a look on the Internet.'

I sighed. I seemed to be doing a lot of sighing lately. Still, at least they'd given up the bath and the pond ideas.

Dad went off to his little office. It wasn't an office at all really. It was just a corner of the front room where he kept the computer. He fiddled and diddled for a while and then he started making some phone calls. After a while he gave up.

'It's very odd, but you can't seem to buy sharks.'

'Oh dear.' Mum was SO disappointed.

Dad suddenly beamed at her. 'But I got something else instead.' Mum clapped her hands like an excited child. A thought struck me. Actually, my mum WAS an excited child. In fact both my parents were children.

Aaargh! How did I end up older than my parents? Well, maybe not exactly

older, but certainly A LOT MORE
SENSIBLE.

Mum was still clapping her hands.
'What did you get, Pa?'

'You'll have to wait and see. It has to
be delivered. It's going to arrive tomorrow
morning.'

'I am so excited!' cried Mum. 'I think
I might burst.'

'BANG!' cried Dad, and burst out
laughing.

See what I mean? Children.

What happened next? Well, we were

woken up by loud noises early the following morning. I pulled back my curtains. There was a large crane outside, one of those cranes on the back of a truck. The truck had a trailer attached to it.

There was something big on the back of the trailer, but I couldn't see what it was because it had a cover thrown over it. The truck driver jumped down from his cab and Dad went out to speak with him. Dad, I couldn't help noticing, was still in his pyjamas and dressing gown. His teddy was sitting in his dressing-gown pocket like a baby kangaroo in its mother's pouch.

'Where do you want it, mate?' asked the truck driver. 'Front garden?'

Dad shook his head and pointed up. 'On the roof.'

The truck driver pulled his baseball hat from his head and scratched his bald skull. 'On the roof? Are you sure? What do you want it up there for?'

'Because that's where it has to go,' Dad said simply.

'OK. You're the boss.' The driver shook his head. Even from my bedroom window I could see he was muttering to himself. Most people start muttering shortly after meeting my dad – or mum, for that matter.

The driver walked back to the trailer. He undid the ropes holding the cover down. Finally he grabbed one corner of the cover and pulled it away. Do you know what was underneath? A rhinoceros. A full-size plastic rhinoceros. Painted pink.

I gazed down at the scene below. Mum went running up the garden path to the gate, also in her dressing gown and pyjamas.

'Oh, it's gorgeous, Pa!' she cried. 'That will look wonderful on our roof.'

Dad nodded and grinned. 'We'll be on the telly for sure,' he said.

The truck driver went to his cab. The engine revved. The crane began to move. Slowly it lifted the huge rhino from the trailer and swung it round towards the house. The crane arm began to extend, getting longer and higher, reaching up into the sky. The pink rhinoceros slowly twirled round as if it was trying to work out where it was going.

Now it was hovering above the roof. Down it came, bit by bit, until CRUMP! Its four fat feet made contact with the roof. The crane hook was disengaged and the arm shrank back to normal size. The driver jumped down from his cab and gazed up at the rhino on the roof.

'Are you quite sure that's where you want it?' he asked.

'Oh yes,' said Mum. 'That's perfect.'

'Right. I'll be off, then.'

As the truck drove away, my parents stood in the garden, gazing up at the pink beast.

'Let's go and phone the TV people,' suggested Dad, taking Mum's arm and steering her back into the house. He went straight to the phone.

'It's been up there since this morning,' said Dad. 'Just a moment, there's a funny rumbling sound . . . I can't hear you –'

The noise was dreadful. It made

the whole house shake. It sounded as
if something ginormous was sliding down
our roof. That was because something
ginormous WAS sliding down our roof.

THE PINK RHINOCEROS!

'Quick!' cried Dad. 'Get out the back!'
We rushed out to the garden and
looked up. We were just in time to see a
giant pink rhino's bottom sliding
backwards down the roof and heading
straight for us.

'Quick!' cried Dad. 'Get back in!'

Faster and faster went the rhino, bringing down tiles with it. Faster and faster in a great scraping roar of noise until it reached the edge of the roof, shot over the gutter and plummeted down, down, down until –

SPLOOOOPPP!

Gigantic blobs of rice pudding came flying out of the pond in every direction as the back half of the pink rhinoceros landed with its bottom fair and square in the middle of the pond. Rice pudding thudded against the house, splattering the door and windows until we couldn't even see out.

At the same time there was a dreadful CRUNCH! from the front of the house. We rushed to the front room and stared out of the window. The rhino had obviously snapped in half on top of our roof and the front half had slid down and crash-landed on to the garden path, blocking our front door.

Silence. Mum and Dad stared at

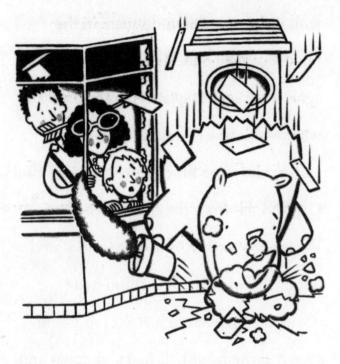

the shattered creature and then at each

other. 'I'll make a pot of tea,' said

Mum sadly.

Dad stroked his chin. 'What a shame. It looked quite good for a few moments, up on our roof.' He shook his head.

'Dad?' I began. 'The front door won't open and neither will the back door. How am I going to get to school?'

5

Mr Jollop Knits a Jumper

I was late for school. Very late. I ran all the way, but my feet kept sticking to the pavement because of all the rice pudding on the bottom of my shoes. I was dreading it. Mr Jollop was sure to want to know why I was turning up at half past ten in the morning.

'Ah, Heathrow,' Mr Jollop began, before I'd even shut the classroom door behind me. 'You're late.'

'Sorry, Mr Jollop,' I mumbled.

'Any particular reason why you're so late?' Mr Jollop asked.

'I couldn't get out of the house,' I said.

'Oh, oh? Really? Why was that?' Mr Jollop's eyebrows were already heading for the knitting needles.

'The front door was jammed,' I explained.

'Oh, oh, I see, all right. So, why was it jammed?'

'It was blocked by a rhinoceros,' I muttered, and the class began to snigger.

'Oh, oh, oh!' went Mr Jollop. I think his eyebrows were starting on an entire jumper by now. 'Blocked by a rhinoceros. Where had that come from?'

'It fell off the roof.' The class was giggling, hands over mouths.

'Indeed? Oh, oh. Um, so did you try the back door?'

'That was blocked too,' I told him.

'I see. Was that another rhinoceros falling off the roof?' Mr Jollop smiled at his little joke.

'No, Mr Jollop,' I said. 'It was the other half of the same rhinoceros – the back half.'

'Oh, oh. Of course. The other half. And it blocked the back door?'

'No, Mr Jollop. The door was jammed shut by too much rice pudding.'

That was it. The entire class was now rolling about the floor, clutching their sides. Meanwhile Mr Jollop's

eyebrows had knitted both sleeves of

the jumper.

'Oh, oh, rice pudding? Goodness,

there must have been an awful lot of it.'

'Thirty cans,' I said heavily. 'Catering size.'

'So the rice pudding was in the cans and jamming the door?' Mr Jollop suggested.

'No, the rice pudding was in the garden pond.' Howls of laughter all round. Mr Jollop was waving his arms about agitatedly, trying to understand.

'But how had the rice pudding blocked the door when it was in the pond?' asked Mr Jollop.

'The other half of the rhinoceros had

fallen into the pond full of rice pudding and squirted it out against the back door.'

'Oh, oh,' sighed Mr Jollop, while his eyebrows started on the front and back of the jumper. It was going to be a very big jumper too. 'I think I need to sit down, Heathrow. Oh, I am sitting down.' My teacher rubbed his forehead hard. 'Do you always keep rice pudding in your pond? I try to stick to frogspawn in mine. Why was your pond full of rice pudding?'

'It was my dad's idea,' I explained.

Light dawned on Mr Jollop's face and all his knitting unravelled. 'Ah! Ah! Your father's idea! Your father – the one with the axe in his head?'

'Yes, Mr Jollop.'

'Oh, ah, yes, now it's beginning to make sense.'

Mr Jollop looked so relieved I felt quite sorry for him. But I was relieved too. At least he understood. Yes, indeed, as soon as he knew my parents were involved, it all made crazy sense.

The class got back on their chairs, but they spent the rest of the day trying to get me to retell the rhinoceros story again and again because they thought it was so funny.

When I got home that afternoon, Mum and Dad had cleared up the mess in the front garden. They had picked up what was left of the rhino's head and put it out at the back with the rest of the beast. The back garden was still a bit sloppy with rice pudding and there were blobs of it halfway up the house wall where Mum and Dad couldn't reach.

'It's taken us all day to clean up,' Mum told me.

'It has,' said Dad. 'I must say I don't think that rhinoceros was very well made, Ma. You don't expect a rhinoceros to snap in half like that.'

'You don't, Pa,' agreed Mum.

'Still, never mind. I've had a new idea.'

My heart sank yet again. Was there no end to this?

'Have you, Pa?' asked Mum with a smile.

'I have. We are going to wear as many clothes as possible. We'll start with our underwear and socks, as many pairs as possible. Then we'll put on T-shirts and shirts and trousers, and you can wear lots of skirts and dresses and then jumpers and jackets and as many coats as we've got. How about that?'

'It's a good idea, Pa,' said Mum. 'We're certain to get on the telly. And you can join in too, Heathrow. That would be fun.'

'I think I'll just watch, thank you,' I murmured. 'I've had enough excitement for one day.'

Dad gave a jolly laugh. 'It has been an exciting day, hasn't it? But tomorrow is going to be even better. Let the cameras roll!'

6

Spot the Cake

Breakfast was rather strange the next morning. Mum was in her pyjamas and dressing gown, but Dad had already got himself dressed. He had to eat standing up because he couldn't bend easily. He was wearing so many clothes, you see.

'I've got seven pairs of socks on my

feet, fifteen pairs of underpants, twelve vests, eight shirts, six pairs of trousers, five jackets, four coats, six scarves and three hats,' he announced.

'You look very red, Pa,' said Mum.

'Bit hot,' Dad admitted. 'I'll be better when I'm outside.'

'Sunny day,' I pointed out helpfully.

Dad pulled at one of his many collars and looked even more uncomfortable. Mum watched him carefully.

'The thing is, Pa, I'm not sure that wearing all these clothes is a good idea.

We're going to be awfully hot. You're

sweating already and you've only been up

ten minutes.'

Dad wiped his brow. 'Have you got a better idea, then, Ma? I thought you wanted to be on the telly?'

'I do,' agreed Mum. 'But you look so uncomfortable with all those clothes on.'

'You were uncomfortable when your bikini filled up with rice pudding,' Dad reminded her.

'I know, Pa, but that was only a bit – clammy. And lumpy. And itchy. You've turned as red as a stick of dynamite and I think you might explode if you keep all those clothes on for much longer.'

'It is,' panted Dad, 'VERY hot in here.'

'Then take them off and we'll think of something else. I had an idea of my own in the night.'

So Dad began to remove most of his clothes, feeling better with each layer he peeled off. Eventually he was able to sit down at the table to finish his breakfast. 'That's better!' he sighed. 'Now, what's this idea of yours, Ma?'

'Well, you know how sometimes when we watch the news on telly, they show someone making the biggest pizza in the world, or the longest sausage – that sort of thing?'

'Yes,' said Dad, shaking his head sadly. 'And I think I know what you're thinking, Ma, but our kitchen isn't big enough to make the biggest ANYTHING.'

'But you're NOT thinking what I'm thinking,' said Ma, a note of triumph in her voice. 'I was thinking I could make the SMALLEST something in the world.'

Dad looked at her. 'What an astonishing idea. No wonder I wasn't thinking what you were thinking. You were thinking quite the opposite of what I was thinking!'

'I was, Pa, I was!'

Dad was getting excited. 'You could make the smallest fried egg!' he suggested, gobbling up the last bits of his own breakfast. Mum wasn't so enthusiastic.

'I'd need to get the smallest egg first, Pa,' she pointed out. 'And that would mean finding the smallest chicken AND getting it to lay one. It's too complicated.'

Dad's face fell. He couldn't think of anything else. 'I suppose you've got a better idea,' he muttered.

'I have, Pa. I am going to make the smallest wedding cake in the world.'

'But how small would your wedding cake be?' asked Dad.

'As small as small as small as I can

make it. It will have icing on the top, but it will be totally teeny tiny.'

Dad nodded. I could tell he wasn't at all sure about this, but I think that was because it wasn't his idea and he couldn't help either. He felt left out.

'I have to go to school,' I told them.

'Have a good day!' said Dad.

'And when you come back we'll show you the smallest wedding cake in the world,' said Mum, beaming away like some merry Fairy Godmother about to turn a pumpkin into a carriage.

*

At school we spent most of the afternoon in the Art Area. Mr Jollop said we could paint whatever we wanted. I painted a picture of a beautiful, clear blue sea, with hardly any waves – just a calm, blue sea. Happy white wavelets trickled cheerfully on to a beautiful beach of soft, golden sand. Beyond the beach, tall palm trees with luscious, fronded leaves swayed gently in the balmy summer breeze.

I completely forgot about home and what was going on there. The painting

left me feeling calm, quiet and relaxed.
I let out a long, slow sigh of pleasure
and went to see what my classmates
had painted.

Every single one of them had painted
a picture of a giant pink rhinoceros
landing in an equally giant bowl of rice
pudding. I gritted my teeth.

When I got home that afternoon, the
house was filled with the smell of baking
and an air of huge excitement. Dad
grabbed me the moment I got in.

'Ma's done it!' he said, shaking my

shoulders. 'She's done it! She's made the smallest wedding cake in the world. They're coming round, this afternoon, here, to our house. They're coming, Heathrow!'

'Who's c-c-c-coming?' I asked. My words came out funny because Dad was still shaking me.

'The newspaper people! And once the telly people see the newspapers then they'll want to come. We're going to be on the telly! We're going to be famous!'

Dad pushed me through into the

kitchen. Mum stood there, patting her hair into shape, her face flushed with success. I glanced around, trying to find the smallest wedding cake in the world.

Mum laughed. 'He can't see it, Pa! Heathrow can't see it!'

'Of course he can't, Ma. It's too small!'

They both burst out laughing. Mum beckoned me over. A small square of white paper was laid out neatly on the side. 'That's it, there,' she said.

'I still can't see anything,' I told her.

'I know. Try using this.'

Mum reached into her apron pocket and produced a magnifying glass. I took it and bent over the paper.

'It's just about in the middle,' Mum said helpfully.

I scanned the paper. Yes, there it was. A tiny crumb of a cake. On top of that was an even smaller crumb. On top of that was an even smaller, smaller crumb. And on top of that was an even tinier dot of white on the top. The icing. It was a three-tier wedding cake, the smallest in the world.

'It is incredibly small,' I agreed, handing the magnifying glass back to Mum. 'But why would anyone want a very small wedding cake? Wedding cakes are supposed to feed lots of people so why make such a small one?'

'Just to show you I can,' said Mum. 'It doesn't have to make sense, does it?'

I couldn't think of an answer to that, but my dad could.

'It could be for a very small

wedding, with very small people,' he suggested.

I looked at him and he nodded back at me. Was he being serious or was he joking? Sometimes it was impossible to tell with my dad. Anyhow, at that moment the doorbell went. It was the newspaper photographer and a reporter too. They came bustling into our little kitchen.

'Now then,' began the reporter. 'We're in a bit of a rush. Where's this amazingly small wedding cake?'

'Yeah,' cried the photographer, clamping bits of his camera together and checking the settings. 'Where's the cake?' He glanced all around, dumping his heavy camera down on the side with a bang.

Right on top of the white sheet of paper.

Mum's scream could be heard half a mile away.

After Dad had hustled the newspapermen out of the house, he took Mum upstairs and put her to bed. He

came back down half an hour later and

sat in the front room with his head in

his hands.

'Can't Mum make another one?'

I suggested.

'She hasn't got the heart for it,' murmured Dad.

I felt very strange. I thought my parents were quite crazy – I mean wanting to be on telly and all that rubbish. They were driving me mad with their daft ideas. But I hated seeing them come so close and have it all taken away – and I mean really taken away, because that crumb of a cake was now firmly stuck to the bottom of that idiot reporter's camera.

And most of all I didn't like seeing them so miserable.

For the first time I found myself
wondering if I could think of something
to get them on telly.

7

Flying High

I couldn't. I couldn't think of a thing. In fact sometimes I wonder if you have to have a special kind of brain to think up those sorts of daft ideas. Obviously Dad's brain could do it, and Mum's brain could do it too. But my brain – well, mine just seemed to be *sensible*.

And now, when I wanted it to go crazy, it wouldn't and I felt as if I was missing something. I began to realize that being sensible was only part of the picture.

To be honest, I did think of one or two things, but they were pretty useless really. I thought Dad could turn the car into a convertible by cutting off the roof. Then I remembered he couldn't even get a fountain gnome to work and converting the car was going to be a lot more complicated than a squirting gnome.

I thought maybe he could build a hot-air balloon. Then I remembered he couldn't even get a fountain gnome to work and building a hot-air balloon would be a lot more complicated than a squirting gnome.

Perhaps he could create the tallest tree house in the world. Then I remembered he couldn't even get a fountain gnome – well, you know the rest.

Besides, those ideas were too ordinary. They had no crazy spark to them. I was discovering that thinking up crazy ideas was a lot more difficult than you think.

So the next morning I went down to breakfast in a gloomy mood, expecting to find everyone feeling much the same way.

'Hey ho, Heathrow!' cried Dad, flashing an enormous smile at me.

'Ready for school?' asked Mum, handing me a plateful of scrambled egg, bacon, toast AND beans.

'You two seem pretty cheerful,' I said.

'That's because we ARE pretty cheerful, aren't we, Pa?'

'We certainly are,' agreed Dad. 'We've been talking half the night and we have come up with a cracker of an idea. We are going to make a flying bed. There! What do you think of that?'

I almost choked on my toast. 'A flying bed? How will you do that?' You see, I was already thinking about that fountain gnome.

'Balloons,' said Mum. 'Lots of balloons.'

'Tied to our bed,' Dad continued.
'Balloons filled with helium.'

I nodded. 'It might work,' I said.
You should have seen their faces. It was
as if I had given them permission to stay
out until midnight. They beamed at
each other.

'He thinks it'll work,' cried Dad.
'And, by ginger pudding, it will! Now,
you get yourself off to school, lad, and
by the time you get back we'll be all
set up.'

It was great to see them fired up

with enthusiasm again and I went off to school rather impatiently because I couldn't wait to get back to see how it was going. All day I sat in class wondering how things were working out back at home. I've told you quite enough about Dad's DIY skills for you to know why I was still a bit worried.

However, when I got home I was in for a surprise. Parked outside our house at the top of the hill was my parents' wooden bed. It was covered with balloons of all colours, shuffling about in the

breeze like lollipops trying to escape a
crowd of lollipop eaters.

Mum and Dad were there beside it,
in their pyjamas. They were still blowing
up balloons with helium and tying them
round the bed. I noticed a pile of old
bricks in the middle of the bed.

'That's to stop it floating away,' Dad
explained. 'It's almost ready to take to the
air. Your mother and I will get in. We'll
toss the bricks over the side and off we go!'

'But where are the telly people?'
I asked.

'Wouldn't come,' said Dad. 'They said someone did the same thing last month over in America. I pointed out that this is in Britain, but they wouldn't listen. Don't you worry, lad, those telly people will soon come flocking here when they see us drifting overhead in our flying bed. Whoa! Did you feel it try to take off then? I reckon we're ready, Ma!'

My parents climbed on to the bed. By this time many of the neighbours had gathered round to watch. They helped me tie the last few balloons to the frame.

Finally Mum and Dad started to offload

the bricks. The bed began to shift from

the ground. The little wheeled feet came

away from the road.

'We have lift-off!' yelled Dad.

'Yippee!'

'Hooray!' shouted the neighbours.

The bed began a kind of dance,

sometimes coming back down to the road

and sometimes lifting a little way into the

air. It began to drift down the hill with

the crowd slowly following.

One or two of the balloons broke away from the bed and soared up into the sky.

'I don't think you tied them on properly, Pa,' said Mum as the bed bumped on to the ground again.

'It might have been you, Ma,' Dad answered crossly, grabbing wildly at a few more escaping balloons and almost falling out of bed as a result.

Now there weren't enough balloons to keep the bed afloat and it came clunking back on to the road for the last time.

However, they were still near the top of

the hill so now the flying bed turned into

a racing-car bed and began to whizz

down the slope. Balloons streamed out behind it with more and more of them being ripped away by the wind or exploding from the pressure.

Faster and faster went the bed with Mum and Dad clinging on for dear life.

'Stop them!' I yelled. But how could anyone stop them? This racing-car bed was going for the world land-speed record. It was careering down the hill straight towards the park at the bottom. And in the middle of the park was the Great Pond.

I raced back to the house, grabbed my bike and set off after them. Soon I had left the chasing crowd far behind, but there was no way I could catch up with the speeding bed. It was travelling too fast and was way ahead of me. I pedalled like fury, faster faster faster!

Ahead of me the bed went clanking and rattling through the park gates and headed straight for the Great Pond where all the ducks were quietly dabbling and quacking and inspecting each other's bottoms.

'Help!' yelled Dad.

'Help!' screamed Mum. 'I can't swim, Pa!'

'Neither can I, Ma!' Dad cried.

I pedalled even faster. My feet were a blur. As I passed between the park gates I saw the bed hit the Great Pond –

SPLOOOSH!

A giant wave of water shot into the air. It was closely followed by an explosion of ducks and geese as they took to the air, squawking and squeaking and flippety-flapping as the bed floated into the middle of their pond.

It was hard to know who was more terrified, the ducks or my parents. The mattress drifted away from the wooden frame, with my parents on it. And then it began to take on water and sink. Deeper and deeper into the water it went, with Mum and Dad clinging to each other, first sitting down, then kneeling and finally standing as the water rose around them.

'HELP!' they yelled. 'SOMEBODY SAVE US!'

I leaped from my bike, grabbed the nearest life belt and threw myself into the water. Urrruuugggh! It was cold – very cold. And full of duck weed. (For the ducks presumably.) I swam out towards my parents, dragging the life belt with me, hoping that one would be enough.

My heart was thundering. My breath was whooshing in and out of me like a tortoise trying to overtake a Ferrari.

'Hurry, Heathrow!' yelled Dad.

I put on a final spurt and reached them just as the mattress finally sank to the bottom and they were left struggling in the water. They clung to the life belt, resting their chins on the top. Together we kicked our feet and slowly, oh so slowly, we headed back to shore. We must have looked like some strange and giant jellyfish wearing pyjamas.

As we reached the edge of the Great Pond and staggered out, several vans screeched to a halt by the park railings. People tumbled out of them and raced towards us, cameras flashing.

Suddenly the place was heaving with reporters and onlookers. Everyone was talking at once. I even noticed Mr Jollop among the crowd, holding an escaped balloon. He looked worried too, as if he thought a rhinoceros might come crashing out of the sky at any moment and land on top of him. It was dangerous to be anywhere near my mum and dad!

The woman next to Mr Jollop shouted out. 'That lad saved his parents.'

The others joined in. 'Threw himself

into the water, swam out to them and saved them.'

'Deserves a medal!'

'What's your name, son?'

'How old are you?'

'What school do you go to?'

On and on they went, with cameras whirring and bulbs popping. Mum gazed back happily at the cameras and waved. 'Hello, Mum!' she said, dripping from head to toe.

The reporters pressed forward. The cameramen closed round us until their lenses were almost poking up our noses.

'What do you think of your son?' they asked my parents. Mum and Dad stood there in their soaking clothes, dribbling and panting from their adventure. Dad's face broke into a broad grin.

'He's champion,' chuckled Dad. 'And he's on the telly too!'

14½ Things You Didn't Know About

Jeremy Strong

* * * * * * * * * * * * * * * * * * * *

1. He loves eating liquorice.

2. He used to like diving. He once dived from the high board and his trunks came off!

3. He used to play electric violin in a rock band called **THE INEDIBLE CHEESE SANDWICH**.

4. He got a 100-metre swimming certificate when he couldn't even swim.

5. When he was five, he sat on a heater and burnt his bottom.

6. Jeremy used to look after a dog that kept eating his underpants. (No – **NOT** while he was wearing them!)

7. When he was five, he left a basin tap running with the plug in and flooded the bathroom.

8. He can make his ears waggle.

9. He has visited over a thousand schools.

10. He once scored minus ten in an exam! That's ten less than nothing!

11. His hair has gone grey, but his mind hasn't.

12. He'd like to have a pet tiger.

13. He'd like to learn the piano.

14. He has dreadful handwriting.

And a half . . . His favourite hobby is sleeping. He's very good at it.

Ask Jeremy

Of all the books you have written, which one is your favourite?

I loved writing both **KRAZY KOW SAVES THE WORLD – WELL, ALMOST** and **STUFF**, my first book for teenagers. Both these made me laugh out loud while I was writing and I was pleased with the overall result in each case. I also love writing the stories about Nicholas and his daft family – **MY DAD**, **MY MUM**, **MY BROTHER** and so on.

If you couldn't be a writer what would you be?

Well, I'd be pretty fed up for a start, because writing was the one thing I knew I wanted to do from the age of nine onward. But if I DID have to do something else, I would love to be either an accomplished pianist or an artist of some sort. Music and art have played a big part in my whole life and I would love to be involved in them in some way.

What's the best thing about writing stories?

Oh dear – so many things to say here! Getting paid for making things up is pretty high on the list! It's also something you do on your own, inside your own head – nobody can interfere with that. The only boss you have is yourself. And you are creating something that nobody else has made before you. I also love making my readers laugh and want to read more and more.

Did you ever have a nightmare teacher? (And who was your best ever?)

My nightmare at primary school was Mrs Chappell, long since dead. I knew her secret – she was not actually human. She was a Tyrannosaurus rex in disguise. She taught me for two years when I was in Y5 and Y6, and we didn't like each other at all. My best ever was when I was in Y3 and Y4. Her name was Miss Cox, and she was the one who first encouraged me to write stories. She was brilliant. Sadly, she is long dead too.

When you were a kid you used to play kiss-chase. Did you always do the chasing or did anyone ever chase you?!

I usually did the chasing, but when I got chased, I didn't bother to run very fast! Maybe I shouldn't admit to that! We didn't play kiss-chase at school – it was usually played during holidays. If we had tried playing it at school we would have been in serious trouble. Mind you, I seemed to spend most of my time in trouble of one sort or another, so maybe it wouldn't have mattered that much.

Bright and shiny and sizzling with fun stuff . . .

puffin.co.uk

WEB FUN

UNIQUE and exclusive digital content!
Podcasts, photos, Q&A, Day in the Life of, interviews
and much more, from Eoin Colfer, Cathy Cassidy,
Allan Ahlberg and Meg Rosoff to Lynley Dodd!

WEB NEWS

The **Puffin Blog** is packed with posts and photos from
Puffin HQ and special guest bloggers. You can also sign up
to our monthly newsletter **Puffin Beak Speak**

WEB CHAT

Discover something new EVERY month –
books, competitions and treats galore

WEBBED FEET

(Puffins have funny little feet and
brightly coloured beaks)

Point your mouse our way today!

It all started with a Scarecrow.

Puffin is seventy years old.
Sounds ancient, doesn't it? But Puffin has never been
so lively. We're always on the lookout for the next big
idea, which is how it began all those years ago.

Penguin Books was a big idea from the mind of
a man called Allen Lane, who in 1935 invented
the quality paperback and changed the world.
**And from great Penguins, great Puffins grew,
changing the face of children's books forever.**

The first four Puffin Picture Books were hatched in 1940 and the
first Puffin story book featured a man with broomstick arms called
Worzel Gummidge. In 1967 Kaye Webb, Puffin Editor, started the
Puffin Club, promising to **'make children into readers'**.
She kept that promise and over 200,000 children became
devoted Puffineers through their quarterly instalments of
Puffin Post, which is now back for a new generation.

Many years from now, we hope you'll look back and
remember Puffin with a smile. **No matter what your age
or what you're into, there's a Puffin for everyone.**
The possibilities are endless, but one thing is for sure:
whether it's a picture book or a paperback, a sticker book
or a hardback, **if it's got that little Puffin
on it – it's bound to be good.**